Nick the Wise Old Cat is offered as a series of life-lesson stories and value messages as seen through the eyes of a "wise old cat" and a nice lady guardian. It is the author's hope that each series will serve as an educational seed that will establish or reinforce cherished values within our children and influence positive developments in their moral and social character.

- Nick the Cat, LLC

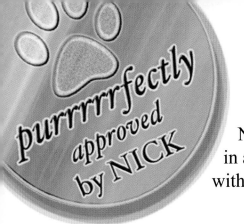

Library of Congress Cataloging-in-Publication Data
Sicks, Linda M.

Nick the Wise Old Cat Series created and written by Linda M. Sicks.
All illustrations created by Dave Messing/All illustration rights owned by Nick the Cat, LLC.

How My Family Changed
ISBN 978-1-936193-02-8
Library of Congress Control Number: 2009935189

Book Design, Marketing and Project Director
Keith D. Ramundo

Printed in China by BookMasters, Inc.
Kowloon, Hong Kong
Printed October 2009
Reference Number A8

All rights reserved. Published by Nick the Cat, LLC.
Printed and Distributed by BookMasters, Inc.
30 Amberwood Parkway, P.O. Box 388, Ashland, Ohio 44805
800-537-6727   419-281-5100   Fax: 419-281-0200
info@bookmasters.com   www.bookmasters.com

Author's Dedication:

Without Nick and Baby Z in my life, I would not have this story to tell.

Without the warm and creative illustrations by Dave Messing, the heartfelt expressions of this story would not have been captured.

Without Keith Ramundo's creative direction, his continuing inspiration, and unlimited patience and humor, we all would have missed out on this wonderful experience.

I am truly grateful for having all of you in my life!

L.S.

Hello, my name is Nick and I am a BIG, VELVETY,
BLUE - GRAY CAT. I have been told I am a wise old cat, for I have seen
and done many things. Let me share with you how my family changed.

HOW MY FAMILY CHANGED

Book Three of Three in Series 1
"The Importance of Family" from the
"Nick the Wise Old Cat" Book Series

T he Nice Lady had taken a new job and she was working many long days. Sometimes she even had to work weekends. While she was gone, I had the house to myself, and I filled my days doing many different things. Often I found myself spending hours watching a sparrow and butterfly play outside while I sat in the sunny kitchen window.

Throughout the day, I nibbled on my food. It kept my belly comfortably full and always put me in the mood for a nice, long nap. When I awoke, I enjoyed taking in a little more window time to see what was happening outside, and to discover whether the sparrow and butterfly were anywhere nearby.

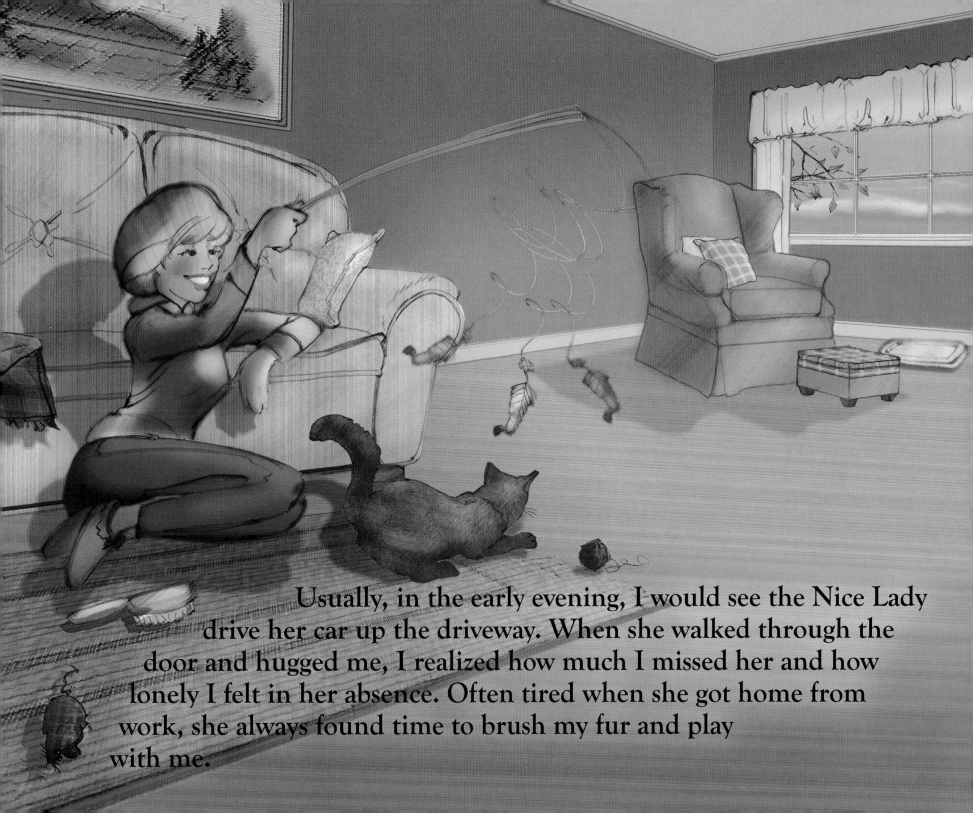

Usually, in the early evening, I would see the Nice Lady drive her car up the driveway. When she walked through the door and hugged me, I realized how much I missed her and how lonely I felt in her absence. Often tired when she got home from work, she always found time to brush my fur and play with me.

I think she could tell I was lonely by the way I followed her around the house. She often told me, "Nick, I will try to make things better for you so that you will not be so lonely while I am away."

One day, the Nice Lady came home while I was relaxing upstairs in one of my favorite napping spots. As she walked quickly towards me, I could see she had something very small cradled in her hands. I wasn't sure what it was, but I could hear some very soft sounds, almost like a baby's cry.

The Nice Lady entered her office and shut the door. Wondering what was going on, I decided to investigate. I tried to look under the door, but there wasn't enough room for me to see anything.

I know, I thought. *I will put my ear as close to the door as I can, and listen.* I could hear her talking, but I wasn't sure what she was saying.

Wait! Did I just hear her say, "You're going to love your new family?" I know that sweet voice of hers. That is how she talks to me! What does she mean by a "new family?" Who is she talking to?

I needed to get in there right away.

I started meowing as loud as I could.

This should get her attention. Oh, I know, I'll scratch on the door. Why won't she let me in? I must see what is happening in there.

Just as I began to let out my BIGGEST MEOW ever, she opened the door and stepped out. She looked at me and said, "I'm sorry to keep you out, Nick, but before I let you in there, we need to talk."

Calming me down by giving me one of my favorite cat treats she said, "I think I have solved our problem."

What problem? I don't have a problem. What is she talking about?

She told me she felt sad about my being home alone while she was away and wanted me to have a playmate.

Playmate, I don't need a playmate! I like having the house to myself. I'm the KING of the house!

The Nice Lady gave me a few more of those yummy cat treats and said, "Nick, remember I told you about the Farm Lady and how she has always been a helpful friend to me? Well, today I went to visit her and all her animal friends.

"Outside by the barn, I told her how I feel about you spending so much time alone."

"As we were talking, the Farm Lady looked at me and said, 'Look around and tell me what you see.'

"I said, 'I see horses, chickens, pigs, and cats.'

"The Farm Lady said, 'That's right, and that's exactly what you need.'

"'Oh no,' I said, 'I can't have all those animals in my house!'

"'Of course not,' the Farm Lady agreed, 'but see how they all have each other as playmates? What you need is a playmate for Nick.'

"The Farm Lady said, 'I have a wonderful idea! Last week, my neighbor brought me a homeless kitten he found wandering in the fields. Out here, everyone knows if an animal needs a rescue home, they can always bring it to me.'

"'This kitten is very little and very shy,' the Farm Lady added. 'I have a feeling he would be more comfortable in a house. Don't get me wrong, he loves being around the other animals here, but I think he could use a big brother like Nick to show him the way and to look after him.'

As I listened to the Nice Lady, I began to think.
Sure I'm lonely at times when she is away, but I don't need some kid brother to look after. And I certainly don't want to share the Nice Lady with anyone. I don't like this at all! I never should have showed her I was lonely. At least then I would still have her to myself. Now I am really upset!

The Nice Lady opened the door and walked with me into the room and said, "Nick, I want you to meet Baby Z."

"'Baby Z,' what kind of name is that?" I asked.

She explained that the markings on his fur looked like the letter "Z," and he was so little, just like a baby.

"Yeah, whatever. Take him back to where you found him. I don't need anyone by the name of 'Baby Z' to be my playmate," I said.

As I turned to walk out the door, I felt something pulling on my tail. It was Baby Z trying to get me to play with him. I looked him right in the eyes, hissed at him, and walked away.

"Nick, get back here," I heard the Nice Lady say. "That is no way to treat our new family member." I knew she was mad by the tone in her voice, so I walked cowardly back into the room.

Looking at me with big sad eyes, Baby Z was sitting in the Nice Lady's lap. All of a sudden, there was a loud knock at the front door.

"I need to go downstairs to see who that might be," the Nice Lady said, "so please be nice to one another until I get back."

Alone in the room with Baby Z, I promised myself I wasn't going to look at him, even though I noticed his eyes filling with tears. He looked very scared.

"What's wrong with you Baby Z?" I asked.

"Why don't you like me?" he answered as he started to cry. He said he missed the Farm Lady and all the animals.

"Even though the Farm Lady and the animals didn't know me very well, they were always very nice to me," Baby Z said. He kept crying and said he felt very lonely and afraid.

Just then I realized I wasn't the only one experiencing change. We all were. It was certainly going to be different for the Nice Lady and me to have a new family member in the house.

But it was going to be very different for Baby Z, too. Away from the farm, he would have many new things to get used to, including our house, the Nice Lady, and me. I was very fortunate to have the Nice Lady and all the love she gives me. Now I knew I needed to share that with Baby Z.

Jumping up onto the chair, I said, "Please don't cry, Baby Z. I am very sorry for how I've made you feel. It's always been just the Nice Lady and me and I was scared how that might change. I thought if I had to share her with you, she might love you more; I don't dislike you, Baby Z. I was only being mean to you because I was afraid, too."

Baby Z stopped crying, and said, "I am very grateful to have a new home, but it is all so new and strange." Baby Z told me he was afraid the Nice Lady would love me more because she and I were already a family.

I told Baby Z not to worry; there was plenty of love to go around in this house.

I said, "Do you know the best part about you being here, Baby Z? I won't be lonely when the Nice Lady is away, and together, we can share our love with her and each other."

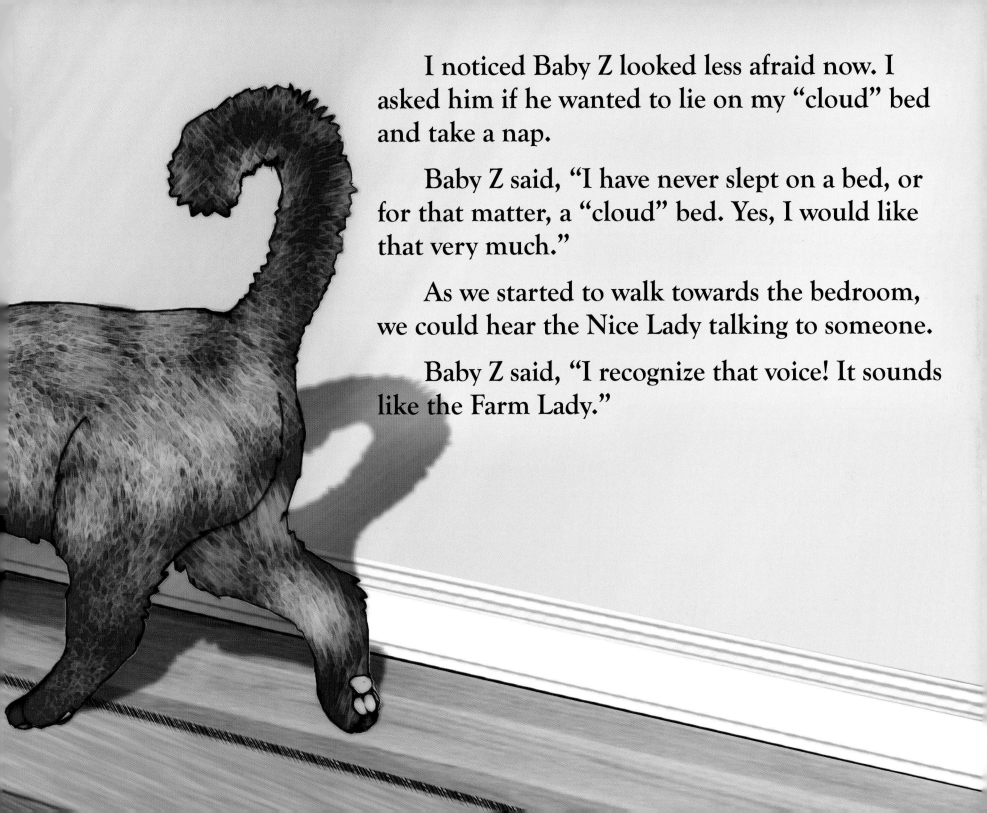

I noticed Baby Z looked less afraid now. I asked him if he wanted to lie on my "cloud" bed and take a nap.

Baby Z said, "I have never slept on a bed, or for that matter, a "cloud" bed. Yes, I would like that very much."

As we started to walk towards the bedroom, we could hear the Nice Lady talking to someone.

Baby Z said, "I recognize that voice! It sounds like the Farm Lady."

Baby Z was right. The Nice Lady and the Farm Lady had come upstairs and were standing in the hallway looking at us as we walked towards the bedroom.

The Farm Lady said she stopped
by to see how well we were getting along.
Looking at me the Farm Lady asked, "Nick,
what do you think of your new playmate?"

I looked over towards the Nice Lady and said,
"I love our new family."

So, as the Wise Old Cat, I have learned through meeting and accepting Baby Z that life is always changing. You never know when or where change may happen, or where it may take you.

Sometimes we like what change brings us. Other times we're not sure we like the change at all.

Change can be scary and sometimes hard to accept. I thought I didn't want a playmate. I was afraid I wouldn't be happy sharing the Nice Lady with a new family member.

But don't be afraid when things begin to change. I now realize as long as you keep your mind and heart open, you might find you LIKE what change may bring.

You could even discover that something wonderful is about to happen!

So always be open to change, and always give change an honest chance to succeed.

Did you enjoy this book? If so, be sure to look for my complete Nick the Cat Series offerings:

- ♥ Series I - The Importance of Family - Publication Date: Fall 2009
  - Book I - How I Found My Family
  - Book II - How My Family Grew Overnight
  - Book III - How My Family Changed

Future Series Topics:

- ♥ Series II - The Importance of Friendship - Publication Date: 2010 - 2011
- ♥ Series III - The Importance of Our International Neighbors - Publication Date: 2011 - 2012
- ♥ Series IV - The Importance of Being Green - Publication Date: 2012 - 2013
- ♥ Series V - The Importance of Helping Others - Publication Date: 2013 - 2014

As with Series I, each of my future series will include three books full of value messages and life lessons for you young readers to grow by and cherish. Each book within each series will be published in six-month intervals which means no vacations for me anytime soon!

- Your friend, Nick

P.S.

♥ Did you know that a portion of the proceeds from the sale of my books will be donated to Adopt a Pet in support of animal rescue in America? Being a rescued animal myself, I can tell you that every donation counts. If you would like to learn more about this very important organization and its mission, visit the AdoptAPet.com website. Also, all rescue shelters interested in fundraising activities through the sale of my books should visit my website, www.nickthecat.com for details.

♥ Kids, for fun and interesting information about me and the Nice Lady – as well as information on release dates for future Nick the Wise Old Cat series books – you too, should visit my website, www.nickthecat.com from time to time. Also, when on my website, you can order my favorite illustrations that I have thoughtfully selected from my books to display in your room for you and your friends to enjoy. These illustrations are available either framed, framed and matted, or on stretched canvas. Each format illustration will be signed by my award–winning illustrator Dave Messing. He is a very "Nice Illustrator."

♥ If you would like to have the Nice Lady read to you the three books on the Importance of Family, then you will love the CD that is also available on my website. Take it along with you when you and your family vacation by car or enjoy listening to it when you are at home. And while you're at it, Nick the Wise Old Cat plush toys can be ordered off my website if you have been unable to find them at your local bookstore.

And, of course, all merchandise available on my website is purrrrrfectly approved by me, as authenticated by my attached seal of approval.

purrrrrfectly approved by NICK

Whether you're reading to your child, grandchild, or the child within, you'll be enchanted by the endearing tales and amazing illustrations of this real-life nice lady and her real, four-legged family member. Endless thanks, Linda Sicks and Dave Messing, for sharing such a wonderful, much-needed affirmation of family — the key building block of society. What a great world this would be if more people heeded Nick's messages!

- Marybeth Dillon-Butler, author of the award-winning picture book
"Myrtle the Hurdler and her Pink and Purple, Polka-Dotted Girdle"